D0090400

THE TRAVELER

THE TRAVELER

Daren Simkin

Pictures by Daniel Simkin and Daren Simkin

FARRAR, STRAUS AND GIROUX

NEW YORK

Farrar, Straus and Giroux
18 West 18th Street, New York 10011

Published in cooperation with Starbucks Entertainment
Distributed in Canada by Douglas & McIntyre Ltd.
Printed in the United States of America
First edition, 2008

Library of Congress Cataloging-in-Publication Data
Simkin, Daren, 1982– .
    The traveler / Daren Simkin ; pictures by Daniel Simkin and Daren
Simkin.— 1st ed.
        p.   cm.
    ISBN-13: 978-0-374-11639-2 (alk. paper)
    ISBN-10: 0-374-11639-3 (alk. paper)
    1. Travelers—Fiction.   2. Quests (Expeditions)—Fiction.   3. Time—
Fiction.   4. Happiness—Fiction.   5. Love—Fiction.   I. Simkin,
Daniel, 1979–   .   II. Title.

PS3619.I5568T73 2008
813'.6—dc22

                                                        2008011513

www.fsgbooks.com
10   9   8   7   6   5   4   3   2   1

For our sister, Shana

Once there was a boy named Charlie.

His mom and dad loved him very much.

He had lots of
friends to play with,

including a girl
with a pretty smile,

and a dog who
took him on walks
all around.

But Charlie wasn't quite happy,
because his life didn't seem perfect.

After all, his parents
made him do chores,

his friends broke
his toys sometimes,

and even his dog
twice gave him fleas.

So one day, Charlie had an idea.
He climbed up to the attic
and pulled out a suitcase.
It was heavy with strong buckles
and could hold a great deal of something important.
Charlie dusted it off and lugged it back to his room.

"What's the suitcase for, Charlie?" his mom and dad asked.

"I'm going to pack up all my time," Charlie said,

"and I'm going to travel until I find something perfect

to spend it on."

"Are you sure?" his parents asked, worried.

"Yes," said Charlie.

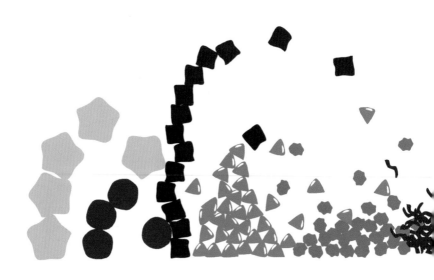

And pack up his time he did:
starting with his big, bulky decades,
then the round, squishy years,
the square, mushy months,
triangular, shiny weeks
and raggedy days,

tons of silky, smooth hours
and crumpled-up minutes.
Charlie squeezed in loads of itsy-bitsy seconds for the journey,
too, even though they didn't seem to want to go.
He closed his suitcase and pulled the straps tight.

And at dawn the next day,
Charlie dragged his suitcase downstairs.
"Goodbye, Mom. Goodbye, Dad."
"Goodbye, Charlie," his parents said with teary eyes.

"Please take my hat," said his pretty friend,
who had hurried over to see him.
And off Charlie went
to find something perfect that would make him happy.

He walked and walked,
and slept and slept
with his suitcase heavy by his side
which made him glad.
Because he could say to himself:

My time is safe in my suitcase,
I can never go wrong—
Soon I'll find something perfect
to spend it all on!

One morning, Charlie walked by a beautiful forest.
Bumbling bees and hoarding squirrels and gobbling turkeys
and even a few wide-eyed deer came out
to see if he would spend his time on them.
Charlie put down his suitcase and considered.

But then he heard a branch fall,
and he didn't want to get hurt.
So the forest wasn't quite perfect, and Charlie shook his head
as he picked up his suitcase and traveled on.

He walked and walked,
and slept and slept
with his suitcase heavy by his side
which made him glad.
Because he could still say to himself:

My time is safe in my suitcase,
I can never go wrong—
Soon I'll find something perfect
to spend it all on!

One day, Charlie walked by a windy desert.
Spitting camels and crawling lizards and bouncing jackrabbits
and even a quiet fox drew near
to watch him make his decision.
Charlie set down his suitcase and thought.

But the sun burned brightly,
and Charlie preferred the shade.
So the desert wasn't quite perfect, and Charlie shook his head
as he picked up his suitcase and traveled on.

He walked and walked,
and slept and slept
with his suitcase heavy by his side
which made him glad.
Because he could still say to himself:

My time is safe in my suitcase,
I can never go wrong—
Soon I'll find something perfect
to spend it all on!

One afternoon, Charlie walked by a sparkling ocean.
Walloping whales and splashing seals and slithery eels
and even the tiny plankton peeked out of the water
to see what he would do.
Charlie let go of his suitcase and pondered.

But he saw the deep water,
and he didn't know how to swim.
So the ocean wasn't quite perfect, and Charlie shook his head
as he picked up his suitcase and traveled on.

He walked and walked,
and slept and slept
with his suitcase heavy by his side
which made him glad.
Because he could still say to himself:

My time is safe in my suitcase,
I can never go wrong—
Soon I'll find something perfect
to spend it all on!

ciao

bonjour

Napaykullayki

Zdravo

Dia duit

As Charlie walked,
he passed lots of jobs
and thousands of books,
countless movie theaters
and musical instruments to play,
all sorts of hobbies and types of sports,
many foreign languages
and wonders of the world.

But nothing was exactly what he was looking for.
Nothing was perfect.
So he kept his time packed up and traveled on.

Until one night, now a tired old man,
Charlie realized he was lonely.
More than anything in the world,
he needed someone to talk to.
Through the darkness he journeyed,
in the moonlight he climbed,
under the stars he trekked.

And eventually he arrived home.
The pretty girl, who was still the prettiest
Charlie had ever seen, was old now, too.
She saw his hat and smiled.

Charlie dropped his suitcase and said to her,
"I have decided to spend my time:
my decades, my years, my months, my weeks, and my days,
my hours, my minutes, and my seconds, too.
I am ready to spend them all, and I want to spend them
at home, with friends. With you."

He unbuckled his suitcase that had held his time for so long and dumped it out.

But only one square, mushy month fell to the ground.

"Where has all my time gone?" Charlie cried.

Although he shook the suitcase and searched every corner, only itsy-bitsy seconds tumbled out.

"Could my time have slipped out of my suitcase?" he asked. "Surely the decades couldn't have—they were so big and bulky! And my years! I don't understand!"

"Charlie, it's not the suitcase that's the problem,"
said his friend. "You cannot save time."
"But," Charlie insisted, "mine was packed up safe—"
and he stopped.
"Is this really all the time I have left?" he asked.
"Yes," she answered.
Charlie didn't know what to do.

"Come sit next to me," said his friend.
She made room for him beside her
in a circle of friends by a crackling fire.
So Charlie sat.

The friends talked about all the marvelous
things they had spent their time on:
beautiful forests,
windy deserts,
and sparkling oceans,
jobs, books, movies, and music,
hobbies, sports, languages, and wonders.

But Charlie, who had passed by all of these, said nothing.
Why am I here? he thought.
Everyone else spent their time.
I didn't.

But just then, someone asked,

"Does anyone know what life would be like if you kept all your time?"

And there was a great silence around the circle.

None of the others had done this, so no one knew the answer.

But Charlie did.

His friend encouraged him to talk about his travels.

Which he did.

And everyone asked him lots of questions,

which he answered.

And he asked everyone lots of questions,

which they answered.

And they all laughed and giggled and joked

and yelled and cried and hugged

as the month faded away.

And as Charlie spent his final itsy-bitsy
seconds on his friends,
he was loved.
He loved.
It may not have been perfect,

but he was happy.